Mystery Of The Pignerol Prison

D.S.Pais

Ukiyoto Publishing

Contents

Chapter 1

There was an infamous prison called Bastille. Baisemeaux was the man in charge of the Bastille. He and Aramis, a priest, and a soldier too had always been friends. But ever since Aramis was promoted to hearing the confession from one of the prominent prisoners of the Bastille, the dynamics of their friendship changed. According to Basiemeaux, Aramis seemed to look like being in a superior position in comparison to his own and thus, had to take his orders.

Baisemeaux leads the way inside the prison chambers. He knows all the routes. He takes Aramis to a prison cell that belongs to the person to whom he must take a confession. Aramis looks at him and that look itself is enough for him to show that he wants to be alone with the prisoner. He gestures to Basiemeaux and is then dismissed.

The prisoner he is about to meet seems like a young man who has low spirits and looks merely as though he simply exists. He anticipates nor waits for anything. There's nothing that he looks forward to and there's nothing that has any hopes left on. He is there as another weight on the planet, awaiting his turn to leave for his heavenly abode, sooner or later.

Despite these conditions, he remains sane through his life in prison, since a few years of his stay.

Aramis asks the man: "Do you need someone to confess your sins?".

The young man has no clue what he needs to confess for, and he doesn't even acknowledge the presence of the person who has entered his cell.

Aramis asks the obvious question: "Wouldn't you want to be free?"

The prisoner remains quiet.

Aramis asks him questions and initiates several conversations, to no avail. The young man seems to not respond to any of this.

Fed up with how the conversation is happening in a very roundabout way, the prisoner finally tells Aramis: "I think both of us can reveal our thoughts at the same time."

The prisoner looks at him but still doesn't want to say anything more than this.

"You distrust me? "Aramis asks. The prisoner nods in agreement.

"'A man's secrets are his own, monsieur,' retorts the prisoner, 'and not at the mercy of just anyone.'"

"A man is bound to make for himself, in the world, that fortune which God has refused him at birth. Being a poor, obscure orphan, I had only myself to look to; and that nobody either did or ever would, take any interest in me." the prisoner says.

The prisoner withholds all information as he has certain conditions. "I want to know how and when the two of us met."

Aramis explains to him: "It turns out that fifteen or eighteen years ago, I accompanied a lady in black silk to visit you."

The prisoner remembers something about Aramis. "You were called the Abbé?"

Aramis says "True!".

The prisoner says: " I know you!"

Gaining some confidence, as Aramis mentions the risk that he has taken to visit him, the prisoner begins to talk to him.

The prisoner has his speculations about the person behind his woes. He enquires about the people with whom he was living before Bastille.

He asks Aramis: "I had a nurse and a tutor. Whatever happened to them?"

The prisoner is heartbroken to learn that his nurse and tutor have left the world.

The advice the prisoner's tutor/father figure gave him before they were separated shaped his worldview. He grew up being told he was unimportant, but how he was confined and monitored suggested otherwise. He was raised with conflicting ideas about his identity and his place in the world, and his tutor's words come back to him at this moment as he considered aligning himself with Aramis.

With a broken heart, he begins to narrate some of the incidents in his life.

"The tutor had received a letter. The letter came from the Queen. Then it flew away and fell into the well." He speaks.

The prisoner pauses for a while and then continues with his story: "They sought a man to go down the well and fetch the letter for them."

"This secret letter mentioned that both my tutor and my nurse were of high rank."

Now it was Aramis's turn. He had to tell his story.

Aramis begins thus: "France has been ruled by King Francis I, King Henry IV, and most recently, King Louis XIII, who is a weak monarch and lets Cardinal Richelieu do most of the actual governing."

"King Louis XIII is married to Anne of Austria. She had difficulty producing an heir. But with time, she produced twin boys. I revealed to you a big secret just now." He pauses. The prisoner doesn't understand.

"King Louis XIII decided on something that had a drastic impact on your life. He did not want to reveal the existence of the younger twin. Eventually, King Louis XIII died. King Louis XIV ascended the throne."

Aramis then hands the prisoner a portrait of the current king - Louis XIV and a mirror.

"Now can you compare the two?"

The prisoner is shocked. They look quite the same.

The prisoner is the twin brother of the ruling King. His name is Philippe. But he knows that there's nothing that can be done, despite knowing the secret.

"I know that there is no hope." Philippe remains unconvinced, hearing Aramis' plans for him.

Aramis plans to swap him for the legitimate king. He has his agenda behind doing it. Once the former prisoner becomes king, Aramis hopes to be the prime minister or even pope.

Aramis kneels before the young prince. He kisses the prisoner's hand before he leaves the prison doors, making a promise to come back for the prince. Despite that, the young prince doesn't keep any high hopes of a bright future.

Aramis taps the prison door. It was time for him to carry out the plan that he had in mind.

Baisemeaux opens the prison door to let the guest out. He then guides Aramis out of the prison.

Chapter 2

D'Artagnan had quite recently received a commission to be a lieutenant.

Realizing he hadn't seen Porthos in two weeks, D'Artagnan heads to Porthos's place.

As he is near the door, he sees Porthos. He is inspecting a fabric that his overweight valet Houston is holding. But he doesn't seem to look happy.

"What happened?" D'Artagnan asks Porthos.

Porthos welcomes the arrival of his friend. As he greets him, D'Artagnan looks around and compliments him on his collection of clothes.

However, Porthos says: "This is nothing but trash."

He further continues: "I ordered up seven suits a week, all in the latest fashion, and Houston continued to be fitted for them."

"However, Houston started gaining weight." He finally remarks and that has caused him displeasure as none of the clothes fit him.

D'Artagnan tells Porthos: "Do not despair." D'Artagnan has the King's tailor, Perrin, in mind and he recommends Perrin to him.

The King's tailor lived on Rue St. Honoré. Perrin's ancestors dated from the time of Charles IX, several hundred years ago. Perrins were expert tailors who became wealthy as they dressed the nobility. Perrin worked for the King.

Carriages upon carriages were waiting, all with the same destination in mind: Perrin.

Porthos despairs, but D'Artagnan points out to him: "If we get out of the carriage and walk, we can gain entrance."

When they get to the door, the two friends find a servant politely turning away all the noblemen who are trying to get an appointment.

 D'Artagnan recognizes Molière and asks him: "Where may Perrin be found?"

Molière tells D'Artagnan: "Perrin is in his rooms but cannot be disturbed."

However, D'Artagnan insists on them meeting Perrin urgently. Molière decides to talk to his master and get back to them.

Perrin is busy examining a piece of fabric but goes to greet the guests.

D'Artagnan introduces his friend in grand majesty and explains his situation.

However, Perrin is not happy with the idea of making a suit for Porthos within two days. But D'Artagnan finally manages to cajole him to get it done.

Thus, Perrin tells Porthos to get measured.

The two of them find Aramis there too.

Perrin, D'Artagnan, and Aramis are left alone in the room. Perrin resumes examining the fabric, and Aramis is annoyed that D'Artagnan hasn't already left.

D'Artagnan then points out that he does not have any business at Perrin's place and can thus leave.

Aramis realizes that D'Artagnan is quite suspicious.

Aramis tells Perrin: "The great painter Le Brun is here. "

Perrin asks: "Would you want the suit made for him like one of the Epicureans?"

Perrin is making a suit of clothes for each of the Epicureans, whom Fouquet plans on presenting to the King as part of a regiment.

However, Aramis is interested in knowing the different suits the King is going to wear.

Perrin is terrified. This is an audacious request.

Perrin is aghast at the idea of giving out information about the King's clothes.

Something is afoot. D'Artagnan's suspicions keep increasing. He keeps thinking: "Why does Aramis want fabric samples?"

Porthos is radiantly happy with this visit to Perrin.

D'Artagnan and Aramis reveal to Porthos that Molière is one of Perrin's chief clerks and a member of the Epicureans.

D'Artagnan asks him: "How did the fitting go?"

The two men leave Perrin's house and continue their conversation about the fitting.

Aramis is in a bad mood. Pelisson is busy writing the comedy "Les Facheux." The other writers are also very busy writing, except for La Fontaine, who is simply wandering around the room.

The two men keep squabbling over rhymes.

Molière asks La Fontaine: "Have you ever fought?"

La Fontaine tells him: "I picked up my sword and told my opponent that the house had been very peaceful since the man started visiting his wife."

Everyone starts laughing at this humor and they continue discussing rhymes.

Before leaving, Aramis stops in to say goodbye to Fouquet.

Aramis leaves with Molière.

Chapter 3

Aramis heads back to Bastille. At about eight o'clock, a courier arrives at Bastille.

Baisemeaux would prefer to continue eating and drinking with Aramis, rather than pay attention to the courier, but Aramis skilfully manipulates him into reading the message.

Baisemeaux gives the order to release Seldon.

Aramis asks: "Did you mean Marchiali?"

Baisemeaux is deeply confused. However, since Aramis has mentioned Marchiali's name, he nods his head.

Baisemeaux releases Marchiali. Of course, he is the Prince, whom Aramis had met before. He has been imprisoned under a pseudo name.

Aramis leaves with the prisoner.

They drive into the middle of the forest so the two can have a proper heart-to-heart.

Aramis takes off the pistols he is carrying.

Aramis proposes: "You both simply exchange places."

Aramis gives Philippe a choice: "Do you want to live a humble life as a private citizen or king of the most powerful country in the world?"

Philippe says: "Give me ten minutes to make my decision."

The prince finally agrees and asks Aramis what he is expecting in return for placing him on the throne of France.

Instead, Aramis wants to prepare Philippe on impersonating the King in court life.

As king, Philippe has plans for everyone.

"Aramis, do you have any other ambitions?" He asks him.

Aramis wants to become the pope. He is convinced that Philippe can rule the bodies of men and that Aramis will take their souls.

Philippe agrees to this plan.

Aramis asks: "Can I kneel before you, Philippe?"

"We ought to embrace. Aramis, you are like the holy father." Philippe says.

The carriage begins moving and heads to Vaux.

Chapter 4

It is perfect. Even Perrin admits as much. The banquet hosted for the King is perfect.

Fouquet confesses to Aramis: "If the King were willing, they could be friends."

Aramis leaves to change clothes.

Porthos is staying next door.

Meanwhile, D'Artagnan is racking his brain trying to understand Aramis's suspicious actions.

D'Artagnan resolves to catch Aramis alone and asks him point blank about his plans.

The King arrives with pomp and pleasure. People keep singing praises around him as a welcome gesture and boost his pride. But he is impatient.

The King is vexed and asks: "Who is responsible for the delay?"

D'Artagnan does not hesitate in pointing the finger at Colbert.

The King gets angry when he realizes that there will be no time left for La Valliere, his current mistress.

Etiquette demands that the King arrives in Vaux accompanied by men carrying shiny pointy objects, but D'Artagnan understands that the King is impatient.

D'Artagnan cuts in with a clever idea and the King is very pleased with this idea.

Chateau de Vaux-le-Vicomte was built in 1655 by Fouquet himself. He hired Levau as an architect, Le Notre to design the gardens, and Le Brun to decorate the many rooms and apartments.

Fouquet observes Le Brun putting the finishing touches on his portrait of the king in his new court suit from Perrin.

The King had arrived with many of his family members. There was King Louis's mother, Anne of Austria, his younger brother, known as Monsieur, his wife Maria Theresa, and his mistress, a woman named La Valliere.

The Superintendent of Finances is Fouquet, who's throwing this party at Vaux to ingratiate himself with the King.

Anne of Austria, the mother of King Louis XIV, was once a powerful political figure when she ruled France as regent when Louis was not yet of age. Her power is currently on the decline and is seen on her face.

Fouquet and his wife personally serve the royals.

Everyone seems to like Fouquet.

After dinner, the King goes to the gardens and takes La Valliere by the hand, and says, "I love you." They spend time with each other.

The evening is complete. The King is taken to the chamber of Morpheus, a magnificent bed chamber decorated by Le Brun.

D'Artagnan visits Aramis's room after dinner.

D'Artagnan tells Aramis: "I beg in the name of friendship, to know the secret."

Aramis plays dumb. D'Artagnan points to Porthos sleeping in the corner and says: "The three of us make an admirable trio."

D'Artagnan does not buy the joke.

However, Aramis continues to play dumb.

D'Artagnan says: "I promise to save my friend."

Aramis swears on their friendship and says: "I am not conspiring against the King."

D'Artagnan accepts this oath.

Chapter 5

Philippe is about to draw away from the peephole when Aramis admonishes him to observe the ritual of preparing the King for bed. Through the peephole, Philippe can see what is going on in the room.

He tells Philippe: "Study the ceremony."

The next day, Vaux is again overflowing with various delights, including a comedy in which Molière is one of the chief actors.

After dinner, the court settles down for a game of cards. The King wins a thousand pistols, and Fouquet somehow manages to lose ten thousand, leaving everyone happy.

The royal party heads for a walk in the park. The King is especially keen to see La Valliere again.

Her love for the King allows La Valliere to see that somebody is in danger of incurring his wrath. La Valliere does not approve and becomes saddened.

The King asks her: "Why do you look so sad?"

She asks: "Why are you sad?"

He tells her: "I am not sad, but rather humiliated by Fouquet's behavior. "

She looks at him questioningly.

He asks her: "Are you on Fouquet's side?"

She says: "No, but what is the source of your information?"

The King beckons Colbert over and insists: "Lay out the indictment against Fouquet. I want La Valliere to approve of my actions."

"I am planning to arrest Fouquet." The King speaks.

La Valliere protests. "It is dishonorable to arrest Fouquet under his roof."

Colbert tries to disagree but fails.

The King, overcome with love for his mistress, kisses her hand.

Colbert despairs, but then remembers he has one more hand to play. As La Valliere leaves, Colbert drops a piece of paper on the floor behind her.

He points it out to the King, saying: "The lady must have dropped it."

The King picks it up as torches arrive to flood the area with light.

The fireworks begin.

King Louis XIV reads the piece of paper, which he assumes is a love note for himself. Wrong. It is a letter from Fouquet to La Valliere proclaiming his love for her.

Chapter 6

The King is angry. His face is swollen red as he goes about seeing the grandeur. It seems to be richer than his palace.

Fouquet notices the change in the King's mood when he comes back to the Party and asks the King: "Any problems, O King?"

The King says "nothing" and heads back to the chateau. The entire court is obliged to follow.

Fouquet assumes the King has quarreled with La Valliere.

The King sends for D'Artagnan. He says: "I want Fouquet to be arrested."

D'Artagnan is astonished. Finally, he asks the King: "Can you give me a written order, you may later change your mind."

D'Artagnan too protests the arrest.

Before he leaves, the King asks D'Artagnan: "Just keep it a private affair."

D'Artagnan says: "It is a rather difficult proposition."

The King then asks D'Artagnan: "Simply watch over Fouquet until the morning, when a final decision will be made."

The King dismisses D'Artagnan, then paces all around his room, fuming.

He now assumes La Valliere defended Fouquet because she loves Fouquet.

The King has a fit, knocks over a table, and throws himself onto his bed.

Finally, the King quiets down and falls asleep.

The bed chamber, slowly starts descending. He is surrounded by men.

The King demands: "I want to know what is going on. "But they don't breathe a word.

The King is now moving in a tunnel. The men ask him: "Follow. If not, you will be rolled into a cloak and carried."

The King follows their orders. He assumes that they have come to kill him.

 It is about three in the morning, when the troupe reaches Bastille. The King is shielded by the men, and kept at a distance where he cannot hear the conversations and is blind-folded too.

Aramis says: "Apologies Baisemeaux for the confusion – it appears that Seldon, was the prisoner that ought to have been released, and I am bringing Marchiali back."

Baisemeaux is a confused man, a simpleton, one who can be fooled by Aramis and wouldn't understand it as well.

Aramis whispers to Baisemeaux: "Marchiali's first move as a free man is to pretend to be the King of France. "

"I am wanting to warn you Baisemeaux that Marchiali is likely to persist in these delusions."

The other masked man with Aramis is Porthos.

Before leaving, Aramis tells Baisemeaux: "No one is to enter the prisoner's cell without express permission from the King."

The King is imprisoned in Bastille. The men leave with Aramis. Baisemeaux doesn't realise anything.

The King, as he lands inside the walls of the prison, gives an involuntary shout, and then fully realizes he is not dreaming, but a prisoner in the Bastille.

Finally, a jailer yells at him: "Be quiet."

He feels guilty that he cannot remember even a small detail about his prison.

A jailer comes in with food and notes that Louis must have been going quite mad to breaking all his furniture.

Louis demands: "I want to see the governor." He threatens the jailer.

The jailer laughs and says: "He is going crazy" He then takes away the knife, that the King was holding.

Louis is left more desperate and angrier than before.

Baisemeaux is annoyed at all the noise as he sits down for his breakfast.

Chapter 7

D'Artagnan shows up at the door of Fouquet.

He has no clue what he can say at this hour, finally, D'Artagnan asks point blank: "Can I spend the night in your room?"

Fouquet is astonished at first, then understands.

Fouquet asks: "Are you forbidden from leaving?"

D'Artagnan continues trying to be tactful, finally admitting the actual reason for him to be there.

Fouquet draws the necessary conclusions and asks: "So will I be arrested tomorrow? Can I speak with Aramis?"

D'Artagnan tells Fouquet: "I will go fetch Aramis. I will be gone from the room for about fifteen minutes."

D'Artagnan leaves.

Fouquet opens some secret compartments and takes out various papers and throws them into the fire.

When D'Artagnan is back, they get into a conversation.

Fouquet talks about his home. He points out saying: "No one in all of France has enough money to buy or even maintain the splendors of Vaux."

Fouquet tells D'Artagnan: "You are a wonderful man, and I am sorry to make my acquaintance so late."

The two of them spend the night peacefully.

Chapter 8

In the morning, Aramis walks into the bed chamber of the King. Philippe is awake and expecting him.

Aramis goes to intercept D'Artagnan and prevent him from entering the bed chamber, where he might suspect something is amiss.

Fouquet asks D'Artagnan: "Can I have Aramis come see me?"

D'Artagnan agrees.

D'Artagnan knocks on the door to the King's bed chamber, half-expecting the King himself to open the door. But it is Aramis who opens the door and D'Artagnan is surprised.

D'Artagnan says: "I had a meeting scheduled for this morning with the King."

The King's voice comes from the bed chamber, telling D'Artagnan: "We can meet later."

This clears up the mystery for D'Artagnan, who assumes that Aramis was in the King's bed chamber to negotiate Fouquet's release.

Aramis accompanies D'Artagnan.

Fouquet is more humiliated than grateful when he comes to know what the King has in mind. Well, the change in mind is caused due to the exchange that happened, with the actual King spending his time at the Bastille.

D'Artagnan asks Aramis: "Can I ask a question?"

Aramis as usual doesn't open up and talks about some other things and diverts the subject altogether.

D'Artagnan buys it, on whatever deviated topics that Aramis is deliberating talking about. And now Aramis is embarrassed. D'Artagnan does not want to leave the room, as he wants to be present in the conversations between Aramis and Fouquet.

Fouquet and Aramis are now left in the room along with D'Artagnan. The two men must catch up on a lot of things.

Aramis not-so-subtle tells D'Artagnan to leave; he obliges.

Aramis explains to Fouquet the entire situation of how he has exchanged the two princes.

Fouquet refuses to see Aramis's actions as divine favor. He is aghast that Aramis has dared to perpetrate this crime under his roof.

Fouquet is an honorable man. He advises Aramis to flee.

Aramis decides to leave Philippe to his own devices but to take Porthos.

After instructing Porthos that they are on a mission, the two men mount their horses right in front of D'Artagnan, who holds the stirrups and bids them farewell.

D'Artagnan muses that in another time it would be said the two men were trying to escape pursuit.

Fouquet hurriedly makes a trip to the Bastille. It takes him awhile to reach the prison gates.

Fouquet walks into the Bastille with Baisemeaux, who is ignorant of the crime he helped commit. He asks for the release of the prisoner.

"I need a signed order from the King to release him." He speaks.

Fouquet threatens him.

Fouquet finally grabs the key from Baisemeaux and tells him to leave.

Inside the prison the King is in a complete mess. During his first few moments in the Bastille, King Louis earnestly believes he is dead and that he is in hell. When the reality of his situation sets in, he breaks the wooden chair in his cell and uses it as a battering ram in an unsuccessful attempt to break down the door.

Louis continues shouting: "I am the King, and Fouquet has put me in the Bastille."

The shouting can be heard, and Fouquet is slowly moving into the Bastille to see the King.

When the King sees Fouquet, he isn't surprised.

The King says: "Fouquet are you here to assassinate me?"

Fouquet corrects him: "I am here to free the King."

Fouquet explains to the King: "You have a twin brother. Your plight currently is due to the malady of two of my friends Aramis and Porthos, but I request you to forgive them one last time. Anyways, I have understood the situation and have come to free you. "

The King says: "I plan to kill Aramis, Porthos, and the imposter twin brother."

Fouquet points out: "We cannot spill royal blood on the scaffold. Aramis could easily have shot you in the forest. Aramis needs to be pardoned on those grounds."

However, the King is adamant. Fouquet releases the King from the Bastille.

Chapter 9

The Pignerol Fortress was occupied by France in 1630.

Life for those who had displeased Louis XIV and were sent to Pignerol Fortress was unremittingly bleak.

Pignerol Prison was an infamous prison, known for all the wrong reasons one could find. The Prison was used for men who were considered an embarrassment to the state. There were only a handful of carefully chosen prisoners who were stationed there.

Pignerol Prison had prisoners like Count Ercole Antonio Mattioli who was an Italian diplomat. He was initially kidnapped and later jailed. He was accused of double-crossing the French. There was a purchase to be made of a fortress. This fortress was quite a significant purchase for both parties. But the Count played games and infiltrated. Thus, Louvois put him in prison. He was jailed because of this key fortress which was on the Italian border in the town of Casale.

There was also Marquis de Lauzun who had become engaged to the Duchess of Montpensier. She was the king's cousin. Their engagement happened without the king's consent and so he had to be jailed.

July 1669

Louis XIV's clerk is summoned for an important assignment. He would have to write a letter to the Prison of Pignerol. It was to be addressed to Benigne Dauvergne de Saint-Mars who was the governor of the prison. Louis XIV dictates what he needs to write in the letter. It's a private room and the letter is dictated in absolute privacy. He raises his hand to dismiss his attendants as soon as the minister is in the private room.

The clerk dips the quill into the ink and starts the letter. He has an artistic way of doing things and sits comfortably next to the king listening to every word that is uttered in a calm poise nodding his head and dribbling the words in ink on the papyrus.

Louis XIV dictates: "Write like this. Write to Saint-Mars. There is going to be a prisoner who is due to arrive in the next month sooner or later.

Louis XIV looks at the clerk and instructs him to leave the name blank. He knows the whose name to add there, and he would thus do it himself.

He then continues: "This is to prevent anyone from the outside to listen in on what's happening inside the prisoner's room. Saint- Mars must see this prisoner only once a day. He will provide food and anything else he needs. "

Louis XIV's eyebrows turn wide. He stops awhile before proceeding with his next set of instructions. The clerk finishes writing and waits for him. After some time, he continues and in a stern voice says: "This prisoner is to be told that if he, were to speak of anything other than his immediate needs he would be killed. "

The clerk suddenly looks at Louis XIV not understanding why such a grave punishment was awarded to the prisoner and wonders what crime he would have committed, but he is afraid to ask any questions in front of the Great Louis XIV.

Louis XIV continues with his instructions: "Instruct Saint-Mars that this prisoner is only a valet, and he wouldn't require anything more than his immediate needs, so there isn't much that he would be demanding if he desires to extend his life on earth. He should be aware of the consequence of his actions if he were to ask anything more. "

The clerk nods and fills the paper with these further instructions. The letter writing goes on for a while until the King is satisfied with what he must mention and asks the clerk to read the letter. The King listens with intention.

"Hand it over to me. "The King says to the clerk and dismisses him. The clerk leaves the ink and the quilt as it is and moves toward the King. He hands him the letter and leaves quietly.

The King now sees the letter and he would write there in the blank space, the name of the prisoner who would be sent to the Prison of Pignerol. The King dips the quill into the ink to write the name – Eustache Dauger.

The name alone has different handwriting compared to the rest of the letter. The King folds the letter and summons the messenger. The messenger is there in no time. "Give this only to Saint-Mars". The messenger gives a low bow and swiftly makes his way on his long journey to the destination that the King has decided for him.

The messenger is on his horse, and he is well-guarded with soldiers. They must ensure that the king's message is delivered despite any dire situation. They finally arrive at Pignerol.

The messenger climbs down the horse and walks towards the prison gates, his horse being well taken care of, to rest after the long journey. He mutters a few words to the Prison guard and after his identity is certified, is allowed to enter the gates of the dreaded Prison.

He waits on a wooden bench to hand over the letter to Saint-Mars. He must wait for long as Saint-Mars is doing his Prison rounds and it would take a couple more hours. He looks around him, glad to see a wooden pot with a tumbler for drinking water. He quenches his thirst with the cool water from the pot and waits for the important man. He had stopped once on the way to satisfy his hunger, somewhere in the village where he had bought food for himself.

The man finally arrives. He acknowledges the messenger, seeing the important scroll of brown papyrus in his hand. The messenger walks towards him and finally delivers the letter. His job is done, and he can now wander among the woods and find his way home.

Saint-Mars arches his brows in a gesture to read and starts reading in his mind the letter that he has received and looks at the name that has been written by the King himself. He palms his hand over the name, as though he could feel the person who had written it. He is startled by the name that's being mentioned. Nevertheless, he makes further arrangements.

With no further instructions given, the messenger strides off, leaving the man with the scroll. As soon as he is gone, Saint-Mars gets busy. He has his men carry out the orders given by the King, and he does exactly what has been stated in the letter.

Chapter 10

Philippe is worried when Aramis fails to show up, but he continues acting like the King throughout all the morning rituals.

At one point in time, he even threatens his mother saying: "I will have Madame de Chevreuse (Anne of Austria's friend) thrown out of France. "

D'Artagnan meets Philippe assuming he is the King.

Philippe demands from D'Artagnan:" Where is Aramis? "

D'Artagnan says: "I believe the King sent Aramis on a secret mission…" . The Captain makes an attempt to remind the King about Aramis. But finds no response from the King and he is left even more surprised.

Anne of Austria usually speaks to the King in a different language whenever she wants to share some details privately. She whispers to her son in Spanish.

But Philippe doesn't understand what she says.

When such a drama is happening in the courtroom, the original King Louis appears with Fouquet at his side. He asks D'Artagnan to immediately arrest the imposter King and hands the orders to him that he had carefully asked his clerk to write the previous day.

Before he leaves, Philippe stares down at his twin brother and mother, trying to shame them for what they've done to him. His mother's position in the kingdom has become weak and she cannot oppose her son's King Louis' orders against his twin brother. She is too confused to react.

D'Artagnan turns to Fouquet who is with the King: "Philippe would have made at least an equal, if not better, king to his brother."He then leaves taking Philippe in custody.

Rumors start spreading that a Marshal of France has been taken as a prisoner. But no one knows the prisoner's identity. It is carried out in complete secrecy.

In his letter to Saint-Mars announcing the imminent arrival of the prisoner who would become the "man in the iron mask", King Louis gives his name as "Eustache Dauger".

There was a family of François d'Or de Cavoye, a captain of Cardinal Richelieu's guard of musketeers, who was married to Marie de Sérignan, a lady-in-waiting at the court of Louis XIV's mother, Queen Anne of Austria.

He was born on 30th August 1637.

The "miraculous" birth of Louis XIV in 1638 came after Louis XIII had been estranged from his wife Anne of Austria for 14 years. He was suffering from tuberculosis and impotence. Louis XIII was gay.

Louis XIV' and his twin were born that year. His twin grew up on the Island of Jersey under the name James de la Cloche.

On the other hand, Eustache Dauger de Cavoye was baptized on 18 February 1639.

Eustache Dauger de Cavoye had been involved in scandalous and embarrassing events, in 1659.

In April 1659, Eustache Dauger de Cavoye and others were invited by the duke of Vivonne to an Easter weekend party at the castle of Roissy-en-Brie. A black mass was enacted, and a pig was baptized as "Carp" to allow them to eat pork on Good Friday.

When news of these events became public, an inquiry was held, and the various perpetrators were jailed or exiled.

Supposedly, the substitute father of King Louis who had left for the Americas returned to France in the 1660s intending to extort money for keeping his secret and was promptly imprisoned. His identity would have destroyed the legitimacy of Louis XIV's claim to the throne had it been revealed.

In 1665, near the Château de Saint-Germain-en-Laye, Dauger de Cavoye killed a young page boy in a drunken brawl involving the Duc de Foix.

Eustache Dauger de Cavoye had also been linked with l'Affaire des Poisons.

There was a surgeon named Auger, who had supplied poisons for a black mass that took place before March 1668.

By 1668, Eustache Dauger de Cavoye was already held at the Prison Saint-Lazare in Paris—an asylum, run by monks, which many families used to imprison their "black sheep".

The King was concerned that Dauger should not communicate, rather than that his face should be concealed. What Dauger had seen or done was a mystery.

Eustache Dauger had also been a valet of Cardinal Mazarin's treasurer, Antoine-Hercule Picon. A native from Languedoc, Picon, upon entering the service of Colbert after Mazarin's death, picked up a valet from Senlis, where the name "Dauger" abounds. Mazarin led a double life, "one as a statesman, the other as a loan shark", and one of the clients he embezzled was Henrietta Maria, the widow of Charles I of England.

Louis wanted to enlist Charles in a war against the Dutch and therefore worried about the subject of Mazarin's estate entering the negotiations. Eustache Dauger, Picon's valet, was arrested and incarcerated for revealing something about the disposition of Mazarin's fortune, and therefore he was threatened with death if he disclosed anything about his past.

The prisoner had also been a valet— to Henrietta of England—who had committed some indiscretion that risked compromising the relations between Louis

XIV and Charles II at a sensitive time during the negotiations of the Secret Treaty of Dover against the Dutch Republic.

King Louis had suddenly and inexplicably fallen out with Henrietta and, since the two had previously been very close, it didn't go unnoticed. There was a link between this event and this valet's arrest under the pseudonym of "Eustache Dauger".

His arrest warrant included a letter from a royal minister instructing jailers to restrict his contact with others and to "threaten him with death if he speaks one word except about his actual needs."

Although the original lettre de cachet authorizing his arrest stated that Louis XIV was dissatisfied with Eustache's behavior, he may not have been Louis's prisoner. He was the one to request the lettre de cachet from the king.

Chapter 11

Porthos and Aramis get away from Vaux as fast as possible. Porthos is puzzled and looks at Aramis questioningly.

Aramis responds: "Our fortune depends on our speed."

In the next post, there are no fresh horses available. Aramis remembers his friend Athos staying close by and thus, rides towards his friend's place for a rest.

When they arrive at Athos' place, Porthos is cheerful, however, Aramis is stressed out.

Porthos brags: "I will soon be a duke."

Aramis asks: "Can I speak to you Athos in private?" Thus, when they get those private moments, he explains their situation to him.

Aramis is convinced. He says: "I can salvage the situation through my allies in Spain. "

Aramis asks him: "Athos, can you join us?"

Athos refuses and says: "No, I can't."

Instead, he asks Aramis: "Can you promise to look after Porthos?"

Aramis agrees to this.

Athos loans his two best horses to his friends.

As Aramis and Porthos saddle up for their departure, Athos is overcome with grief and hugs his two friends' goodbyes.

He tells his son Raoul: "I believe it will be the last time I will see my friends."

As soon as they depart, Athos has a visitor. They start having some drinks and refreshments.

"Raoul you can join the conversation. "Beaufort says looking at the young man. Beaufort is the visitor who has just arrived.

Beaufort takes a sip, then offers his glass to Raoul, saying: "My glass bears good luck. Raoul makes a wish."

Raoul tells Beaufort: "I wish to accompany you to Africa."

Beaufort looks at an upset father and says:" Raoul will be my aide-de-camp and will be treated like my son."

Raoul tells Beaufort: "If I am planning on having this exchange with the King, it will be untrue, for I will not serve the King."

But Raoul reveals his plan and says: "I will become a Knight of Malta and serve God instead of the King."

Thus, father and son depart.

They soon arrive at Monsieur de Guiche's residence but are informed he is with the King's younger brother, Monsieur.

Monsieur de Guiche's mistress knows La Valliere. She goes after Raoul and says: "Talk with her in her apartment where you both can have some privacy."

She sends word to de Guiche that Raoul is waiting to speak with him, then asks Raoul: "Are you angry with me?"

Raoul is quiet.

Then another secret door opens and de Guiche enters.

When it's clear that Madame is still nervous about uncovering the affair, Raoul tells her: "I am leaving France soon, and unlikely to return."

De Guiche says: "I am upset to learn that you are going to Africa."

Raoul tells de Guiche: "You are fortunate to be loved."

Raoul cannot bring himself to say La Valliere's name, but he makes his friend swear: "Can you defend La Valliere in the coming years?"

De Guiche agrees to this.

Raoul and his father then pay a visit to Planchet to find out D'Artagnan's whereabouts.

Athos shows up at Planchet's grocery to find all the employees amid taking an inventory.

Planchet tells Athos: "I am selling my business and moving to the country."

Planchet points out: "We should talk in better quarters."

As they enter Planchet's home, they have an interruption. They must wait for the woman.

Once the woman, whose name is Tauchen, has had time to get dressed, the men go back inside.

"D'Artagnan has disappeared," Planchet says bluntly.

After a little coaxing, Planchet confesses: "D'Artagnan did visit the grocery the other day and spent some time consulting a map."

They dig more details from Planchet and conclude where he could be.

Their only remaining errand is to visit the palatial residence and sort out all the details for departure.

Like Planchet, M. de Beaufort is making an inventory of all his belongings. It turns out that he owes almost two million, so he is trying to sell off and give away all his belongings, and then borrow even more money so he can finance the expedition to Africa.

He says: "Raoul will leave before me as far as Antibes. He will need to prepare the army for deployment in two weeks."

Father and son head out, deciding that the whole expedition is just to satisfy the vanity of M. de Beaufort.

Raoul begins assembling a fleet, but one fisherman says: "The ship is currently in the shop."

Father and son get suspicious and ask the fisherman for an explanation. He concludes thus: "I disagreed, and the gentleman again tried to use force. There was a bit of a fight when the gentleman drew his sword. Then the carriage case opened and a phantom with his head covered by a black helmet emerged and threatened us. The two of us fishermen jumped out of the boat and swam for shore. Eventually, we recovered the boat, but there was no trace of the travelers."

They dismiss the fisherman and directly head towards the place where they can find D'Artagnan. They find the castle which has Philippe imprisoned.

A plate with some inscription is thrown out of the castle.

He explains to them hurriedly: "The governor of the castle will kill you both if he believes you have read the inscription on the plate."

D'Artagnan introduces them to the governor of the fortress: "The men are Spanish naval captains."

D'Artagnan tells the governor: "The Spaniards are here to take in the sights."

In privacy, Athos and Raoul tell D'Artagnan: "This visit is a good-bye visit because Raoul will soon be fighting in Africa."

Athos reveals to D'Artagnan in secrecy: "I cannot bear to see my son die."

D'Artagnan says to Athos: "He might yet be saved."

D'Artagnan goes to talk to Raoul.

Raoul asks D'Artagnan: "Could you possibly forward a letter to Mademoiselle de la Valliere?"

D'Artagnan smiles.

Raoul replies: "I can never see her again then because I want to love her forever."

D'Artagnan suggests: "Shorten the letter to: "Mademoiselle: Instead of cursing you, I love you, and I die."

Raoul agrees with D'Artagnan's editorial suggestions and asks D'Artagnan: "Just make sure the letter makes its way to La Valliere after I am dead."

The prisoner in the castle - Philippe has started screaming: "I would like to be called Accursed."

D'Artagnan then receives a letter from the King ordering him back to Paris.

Chapter 12

Athos and Raoul return to Toulon.

Athos gives his son some military advice, and makes his son promise: "Think of me if you are in trouble."

Athos tells his son: "The two of us love each other so dearly that when we part, parts of our souls must also part."

He calls Grimaud, his valet, and tells him: "You must not leave him alone". He thus gives him the services of Grimaud.

Beaufort prepares to leave and tells Athos: "Meet me in Paris."

In the other part of the world, Madame is ill, de Guiche is out of town, Colbert is happy, and Fouquet is ill.

La Valliere is sitting in the center of several ladies, who begin peppering her with questions.

One of the ladies tells La Valliere: "Your rejection of Raoul must be a great sin on your conscience."

La Valliere walks away. She sees D'Artagnan who has just arrived.

She asks D'Artagnan: "Why do you want to speak with me?"

D'Artagnan confesses: "My message is already aptly conveyed by Mademoiselle de Tonnay-Charente."

After a couple of conversations, D'Artagnan sees the King. La Valliere disappears as the King begins to talk.

The King tells D'Artagnan: "Place a guard at the door of each of my chief advisers."

"Fouquet is ill. His health is deteriorating." D'Artagnan says and leaves the King to carry out his orders.

Fouquet is at his residence and is having supper with his friends.

Fouquet says: "I can compare our current meal to Jesus' last supper."

He points out: "I no longer have very much – only powerless friends and powerful enemies."

Pelisson suggests: "You flee to someplace like Switzerland."

As a lot of his money has been seized by the King, his friends toss various valuable pieces of jewelry in a hat so he can have some type of funds.

Fouquet has decided to take the waters.

The rowers exclaim: "Behind us, and rapidly gaining ground, is a boat with twelve rowers!"

The rowers tell Fouquet: "The boat is certainly from Orleans."

Fouquet commands the rowers: "Stop!" He wants to see the boat for a while to decide on his next course of action.

Fouquet orders his men: "Begin rowing again."

He orders the rowers: "Row closer to shore and pretend that I will disembark."

D'Artagnan shows up. He asks: "Is it now time for the arrest?"

D'Artagnan reassures Fouquet and tells him: "When the time comes, I will announce my intentions loudly."

Using very careful language, D'Artagnan tells Fouquet: "This order goes into effect only once the King has arrived, and you should bolt immediately and make for Belle-Isle."

D'Artagnan comes by again, saying: "The King is inquiring after your health." Saying this, he departs.

But it is already too late. The King has arrived too. He asks for D'Artagnan.

"Take Fouquet in a special carriage." The King orders.

D'Artagnan admits to the King: "I tried to save Fouquet. But now I will execute your orders." The King dismisses him, and he goes after Fouquet.

Fouquet requests D'Artagnan to shoot him: "I will then suffer less this way." He speaks.

D'Artagnan also begs Fouquet: "Kill me, I want to die bravely."

Fouquet's house is also searched, by none other than his staunch enemy Colbert. Upon questioning Colbert replies: "I acted for the good of the King."

D'Artagnan further admits: "Fouquet would never attempt escape while I am his guard, but that I would deliberately do a poor job guarding Fouquet."

Colbert explains himself by saying: "Fouquet has been holding me back from greatness."

D'Artagnan asks Colbert: "Can you intercede with the King on Fouquet's account?"

Colbert points out:" The King has his grudges against the man."

The King calls for D'Artagnan and says: "Select twenty men as a guard for Fouquet, who is destined for the Bastille."

Since 1659, the Bastille had individuals who were been locked up, banished into exile, or simply tried within the limits of Paris because of a lettre de cachet.

Chapter 13

At Belle-Isle, Aramis and Porthos are walking around the island, and discussing the curious disappearance of all the fishing boats.

Porthos confesses: "I am unhappy at Belle-Isle and would much rather be in France."

Aramis tells Porthos: "We could have left had you not sent out the two remaining fishing boats."

Porthos then asks: "What about the orders you have been issuing, which are to hold Belle-Isle against the usurper of the throne?"

Porthos tells Aramis: "Sit down on a rock and explain the full story to me." Aramis begins to start with the narration.

They see someone. It's the captain. He says: "I want to see Aramis. I am the captain of one of the two fishing vessels that Porthos had earlier sent out in search of its lost companions."

The captain tells Porthos and Aramis: "All the fishing vessels have been captured by the royal fleet, which has set up a blockade around the island. "

He further continues: "The fleet is under the command of D'Artagnan, who is sending you both a letter through me."

Aramis warns: "It may be a trap. "

Porthos is confused. He needs some explanation.

Aramis explains: "Rather than supporting the real king, we have been working for the false king, and you and I are to be considered rebels against the crown."

Aramis tells Porthos: "We may have to defend ourselves against D'Artagnan. "

Aramis says: "I will stay at Belle-Isle and fight. "

When they are at their discussion, D'Artagnan arrives with some of his men.

Aramis suggests: "D'Artagnan, take Porthos away and explain to the King that he had nothing to do with the crime."

D'Artagnan comes up with a good idea and whispers it to Aramis, who proclaims: "This is infallible."

D'Artagnan announces: "The fleet must return to Nantes with me. "The others who had accompanied him, join him.

Aramis relates D'Artagnan's plan to Porthos.

Aramis tells Porthos: "If there is only time for one of us to escape, you should go."

Porthos retorts and tells Aramis: "We will either escape together or remain together."

Aramis finds Porthos gloomier than necessary.

Aramis asks: "However, I would like to know the cause of your gloom?"

Porthos says: "I am drawing up my will. I feel tired, and that is a bad sign in my family."

Porthos tells Aramis: "My grandfather was twice as strong as me, but that one day when he was about the age I am now, he felt a weakness in his legs as he set out to hunt."

He continues thus: "My father was just as strong as me. He then insisted on going down into the garden, but while on the staircase he fell and hit his head. He died."

Aramis tells Porthos: "These do not mean anything; you are still strong."

Porthos tells Aramis: "I too have felt a weakness in my legs, and I know that my time is coming. I have lived a good and rich life."

Aramis tells Porthos: "You still have years to live. Besides, D'Artagnan is securing our escape right now. Your legs must be better."

The search for Aramis and Porthos has begun.

Porthos seizes a man just then, while he is talking to Aramis. Aramis laughs.

Porthos points out: "I seized the man with my arms."

Porthos suggests: "Let's invite the man to supper and give him lots of alcohol."

The prisoner is nervous at first as he tells them: "The plan is for killing during the fighting, and, if taken alive, for a hanging afterward."

He asks: "Were you both once Musketeers in the King's service?"

The prisoner seems familiar. Porthos and Aramis are pleased to know that it is Baccarat.

Baccarat tells Aramis: "I may have saved the inhabitants of the isle, but the lives of you and Porthos are still at stake."

The servants begin placing rollers under the boat in preparation for the move, but before they are finished a pack of dogs enters the grotto. The six dogs are killed, but there are still sixteen masters left.

They release Baccarat.

Aramis confides in Porthos later: "We ought to shoot him first since he can recognize us."

Each of the men calls for the dogs but gets no answer.

Baccarat who has now joined these men tells them: "I will go investigate the grotto. "

Baccarat is taken aback when he is caught again by Aramis.

Baccarat swears: "I will not tell my companions what happened. I will try and stop them from similarly entering the grotto."

Baccarat returns to his friends and is very reticent about what he has seen in the grotto.

Baccarat waits while his friends enter, and there are sounds of gunfire.

He still lives.

Baccarat tells them: "The men in the cavern are prepared to fight to the death unless the captain can offer them good terms."

The captain asks: "How many men are there?"

Baccarat asks the captain: "Do you remember when four Musketeers held the bastion against an entire army.?""

The captain does remember, and Bacarrat tells him: "Two of those men are in the grotto."

Baccarat makes one last plea: "Let the men go. Leave them alone. "

The captain points out: "I will look ridiculous if I order the retreat of eighty men in the face of two."

Baccarat begs permission: "Can I be part of the first group to enter the grotto?"

The captain allows.

Baccarat refuses to take his sword.

As for the defenders, they have begun to move out of their boat.

Porthos suggests: "Let's hide behind a pillar with an iron bar that we can use to bash in their heads."

Aramis says: "It's a great idea, but we need a weapon that will take out dozens at once."

Aramis tells Porthos: "Wait for my signal."

Baccarat calls his friends onwards, and Aramis tells Porthos to strike.

The bar annihilates the first platoon with no problems.

The soldiers die. Baccarat dies first as he is without a weapon.

Soon Porthos is hurt badly as a ball of something heavy strikes him. He breathes his last saying: "Too heavy."

However, Aramis escapes.

The men row towards Spain as Aramis sinks into silent, immovable grief.

The men soon realize they are being chased, but do not disturb their master until an hour has passed.

The ship continues its pursuit, and the sailors are afraid.

Aramis spends the night leaning on the rails, and one of his men later notices that the wood upon which Aramis's head rested is soaked with moisture.

The moisture was the first tears Aramis ever shed. It was equal to any epitaph Porthos could have received.

Chapter 14

D'Artagnan is deeply upset when he returns to Nantes and seeks a meeting with the King straightaway.

M. de Lyonne comes out, and D'Artagnan tells him: "Tell the King that I am resigning."

D'Artagnan asks: "Am I being arrested?"

Gesvres tells him: "The King wants to speak with you."

D'Artagnan is disappointed in the quality of the Musketeers that the King has currently chosen, who are just not up to the mark as his friends.

He argues with the King: "Officers of the expedition were given lots of differing orders, while I was kept in the dark."

The King says: "The orders were given to those who were judged faithful."

The King then argues: "My actions are accountable only to God, and that I am not the type of king who is easily led by my subordinates as past kings were led."

D'Artagnan argues: "The two men in question were my best friends."

The King says: "Your friends were rebels whom I wanted to be captured. You failed the test."

The King tables these considerations to explain "absolute monarchy which means, "what the King says is law, period."

Louis says: "I am founding a state in which there shall be but one master."

D'Artagnan doesn't respond but doesn't like what the King says.

The King tells D'Artagnan: "Find another guy to serve if you want to manipulate your master."

Then the King tells D'Artagnan: "I will forgive this one breach."

D'Artagnan tells the King: "You are underestimating Porthos and Aramis."

The King asks D'Artagnan: "Is there another king of France?"

D'Artagnan reminds the King: "I came to his defense on the day Philippe was in the room. "

D'Artagnan promises: "My friends will not be taken alive."

The King then points out: "I am the absolute master of France; You will experience either the royal anger or the royal friendship."

D'Artagnan claims: "Being captain of the Musketeers will no longer carry the same kind of glory and responsibility that it once did. "

Finally, he tells the King: "I will cooperate."

The King thanks D'Artagnan, then tells him: "You will be sent into foreign fields to attain the marshal's baton."

D'Artagnan begs the King: "Please pardon my two friends."

D'Artagnan arrives back in Paris after going to Belle-Isle and discovering no trace of his friends.

D'Artagnan asks: "Why was I not informed?"

The King says: "I wanted you to find out for yourself. "

The King admits: "Aramis had sent you a letter recapping the situation."

D'Artagnan admits" You are the only man who could dominate over my friends."

The King mentions: "I could easily have Aramis killed in his hiding place in Spain, but since I am generous, I desist."

D'Artagnan doesn't believe the King's advisers, who were always against his friends out of sheer jealousy.

The King admits: "Colbert advised sparing Aramis's life."

D'Artagnan asks the King to receive three petitioners who were waiting for a long time in the antechamber. They were the friends of Fouquet: Gourville, Pelisson, and La Fontaine.

The three men were weeping.

The King remains expressionless as the three men file in with faces contorted by grief.

The men can't get it together to speak, and the King gets impatient. He tells them: "There is no hope of pardoning Fouquet."

Pelisson finally speaks. "We are there on behalf of Madame Fouquet, who has been abandoned and destitute since her husband has fallen out of favor."

The friends ask: "We need permission to loan her two thousand pistoles."

The King permits them and they leave.

The King then gives D'Artagnan permission to see to the affairs of Porthos.

Mousqueton, Porthos's servant, has lost plenty of weight in two days; his clothes hang on his frame.

Porthos will first details all his worldly possessions, then leaves everything to Raoul de Bragelonne, who he considers his son.

D'Artagnan is left alone to contemplate his friend's last will, which he judges to be admirable.

Chapter 15

Back on his estate, Athos has been preparing for his death.

He stops speaking. His physician comes to check on him.

At one point, he can bear it no longer and goes directly up to Athos and begs him: "Do you mind getting well?"

Athos tells the doctor: "Do not worry —I will remain alive if Raoul is alive. My soul is prepared; I am waiting for news about Raoul."

His mind wanders and Athos gets a vision. The vision disappears and servants come running in with a letter from Aramis relating to Porthos's death. Athos is full of grief, but due to his weakness, he is not able to go for his funeral.

Athos is in bed the whole day and is unable to get up. Mail is delivered for the day, but there is nothing for Athos.

A man on horseback arrives and ascends the stairs.

It is Grimaud.

Athos knows. He simply asks: "Raoul is dead?"

Grimaud answers in the affirmative.

He gets a copy of the letter Beaufort wrote to Athos; a letter that arrived too late.

In the letter, Beaufort asks Raoul to take note since he has promised Athos, that he would bring him back alive.

In the war, they aim at the horse but don't shoot for fear of hitting Raoul instead.

Raoul continues foot toward the fort. He then gets deeply injured.

Later that night, an assistant finds Raoul dead on the ground, clutching a lock of fair hair to his heart.

Grimaud has brought Raoul's body back with him.

Athos upon hearing the news, breathes his last.

At the funeral, La Vallerie is also present.

D'Artagnan shames her mercilessly, saying: "It is you who put both men in their graves."

She says: "I left the court as soon as I heard of Raoul's death, hoping to beg forgiveness from the father, and wound up arriving just in time for the funeral."

D'Artagnan repeats Raoul's feelings to La Valliere: "No one could have loved you as he did."

She tells D'Artagnan: "I will never be able to love without remorse. I could not help but love Louis, but now I will suffer from Raoul's love for me."

Chapter 16

Fouquet's cell was above that of Lauzun in the Pignerol Prison.

Saint-Mars had to give an account of the prisoners to Louvois. Louvois would correspond with the king using letters that he had sent from his encounters with the prisoners at Pignerol Prison.

Saint-Mars wrote to Louvois: "Dauger is a quiet man. He gives me no trouble. He is well disposed to the will of God and the king compared to his other prisoners who are always complaining. Other prisoners constantly try to escape and some of them have gone mad. But Dauger is indifferent to the circumstances he is in. "

When Louvois read the letter, he is in awe of this indifferent prisoner.

Eustache Dauger was taken in stages with a small escort to Pignerol, a journey of some three weeks. Here, he was placed into the care of Saint-Mars, a former sergeant of the musketeers.

Saint-Mars had followed the instructions given by the King. He was ordered to prepare a special cell for Eustache, closed behind 3 doors and so situated that the prisoner could not be heard if he tried to cry out or otherwise draw attention to himself.

In the meanwhile, the King pardons Aramis for his misdeeds after his conversation with D'Artagnan. At least the King keeps his promise with D'Artagnan and spares Aramis' life.

Aramis and Saint-Mars are known to each other. Aramis arrives with another man. It is Louvois who is very eager to meet Dauger. Aramis wants to spend a moment with Dauger and asks of Saint-Mars to meet him. Saint- Mars agrees to this disposition, Louvois waits with Saint-Mars, while Aramis meets the prisoner. He enters the prison where Dauger is seen in a corner.

'By weakness, which, in princes, is always treachery.'" Aramis begins.

Aramis asserts: "Weakness in princes is treachery because of the threat a prince may pose to the throne."

Dauger was isolated at times. The important prisoners, the wealthy prisoners usually had manservants. But Dauger (Philippe) mistaken to be a valet did not have any such luxury.

Aramis leaves him, whispering something in his ears.

Aramis comes back again with Louvois. As they are having a conversation with the prisoner, Aramis observes Louvois. His conversations begin to stagger, and he soon falls asleep.

Philippe exchanges his clothes with Louvois. Aramis and Philippe walk out of prison in haste, bidding farewell to Saint-Mars, before he discovers the exchange. But then, there is no chance of discovering the exchange, since the man will always be wearing an iron mask.

Aramis has plans for Philippe, but for now, he is only concerned about Philippe's safety.

When Louvois learns about the trickery of Aramis, he screams and bangs his head against the walls of the Prison, but no one would listen to his cries. He thus becomes the Man in the Iron Mask.... fate has taken a complete overturn... the content one, issuing strict orders for people to be put in prison is now in the same wretched prison. He curses his fate.

Chapter 17

Four years later, there was a bird hunt in Blois (Athos's land), which was organized for the King.

D'Artagnan is close by. The falconer mentions:" You must be tired after the long journey from Pignerol."

D'Artagnan promptly disagrees, saying: "Fouquet is an honest man."

The falconer says privately to D'Artagnan: "Greyhounds are in fashion these days, otherwise the captain of the greyhounds would never have dared be so impertinent."

He tells the falconer: "I have been away for a month since the death of Anne of Austria; I am not up on all the latest gossip."

He says: "You will meet an old friend at dinner, the Duc d'Alméda, better known as Aramis."

The King arrives with his family members and they start talking.

Madame mentions, delicately: "I thought about complaining to my brother Charles (that would be King Charles II of England)." She talks about a woman.

Madame tells the King: "The Chevalier de Lorraine, despite being my husband's best friend, is my mortal enemy. "

"I will exile Lorraine, and in return, you will help me form a political alliance with England." The King says.

Madame says: "I will visit England with Mademoiselle Kéroualle to cement the alliance."

The King says: "Basically, I hate the Dutch and want to make sure no one will interfere if I wage war with them."

Madame says: "I agree to do it providing my husband consents."

He says: "I want assurance that Spain will remain neutral if France wages war with Holland."

Colbert has his discussion with D'Artagnan and he confesses: "The navy actually has thirty-five vessels and will be increasing soon."

He confesses: "I have also been buying supplies from the Dutch.

English and French navies sailed together for Holland.

Aramis installed Philippe as the King of Spain quietly, after their escape. The young lad had quickly learned the foreign language. All this was done in secret and the twin brother King Louis nor anyone else knew anything about this.

Meanwhile, Madame de Montespan increases in the King's favor while La Valliere becomes increasingly marginalized.

Chapter 18

"Fouquet is served by a man called La Riviere. It is difficult to find men who would serve these high-profile prisoners, as these servants would become as many prisoners as their masters. People are unwilling to volunteer to do these kinds of jobs that kept them with the prisoners. "Saint-Mars's letter to the king began. The King has no clue about the whereabouts of Louvois and has found another minister who replies to all the letters to Saint-Mars.

Then he adds: "I need your permission for Dauger to act as a servant for Fouquet. "

Eustache was described as 'only a valet', and this was reflected in his prison experience.

Saint-Mars very soon receives a reply from the King.

"Dauger must serve Fouquet only while La Rivière is unavailable. He is not to meet anyone else; for instance, if Fouquet and Lauzun were to meet, Dauger should not be present."

Thus, Dauger (Louvois)begins to serve Fouquet whenever La Riviere was sick. Dauger always had to wear a mask when he was serving as a valet. Thus, the interaction between Fouquet and Dauger wasn't a big deal at all.

The King did not want him to spread rumors about Dauger. He did not want anyone to know about Dauger's existence, after all, it was a matter of his throne. He did not want Lauzun to spread any secrets he might have come to know in his interactions.

There was a letter dated 20 June 1678, full of self-pity, sent by the actual Dauger de Cavoye to his sister, the Marquise de Fabrègues, in which he complains about his treatment in prison, where he had already been held "for more than 10 years", and how he was deceived by their brother Louis and by Clérac, their brother-in-law and the manager of Louis's estate.

Affair of the Poisons was a notorious scandal of 1677–1682 in which people in high places were accused of being involved in black mass and poisonings.

Fouquet had a fellow prisoner Count Ercole Antonio Mattioli (or Matthioli).

The best the king would do, however, was to send a letter to the head of Saint-Lazare on 17 August 1678.

Eustache Dauger de Cavoye was still there in 1680, while "Eustache Dauger", the man in the mask, was in custody in Pignerol, hundreds of miles away in the south.

Fouquet dies in 1680. After Fouquet's death, Dauger was kept in close confinement with another man who had also served Fouquet.

However, there is a startling discovery. While Saint-Mars goes to see the body, he discovers a secret hole. He sends his people to find out where the secret hole would lead to. As one of his men passes through the hole, it ends at Lauzun's cell. The secret hole was between Fouquet and Lauzun's cells. Saint-Mars comes to know that these two had communicated through this hole without detection by him or his guards. Lauzun would have been made aware of Dauger's existence.

Saint-Mars immediately sits down at his desk to pen a letter to the King. He had to know what to do and what would be the next plan of action for him.

The King provides clear instructions in a letter immediately.

In a letter sent by the King to Saint-Mars on 10 July 1680, a few months after Fouquet's death in prison while "Eustache Dauger" was acting as his valet, the minister adds a note in his handwriting, asking how Dauger might have had certain objects found in Fouquet's pockets—which Saint-Mars had mentioned in previous correspondence, now lost—and "how he got the drugs necessary to do so".

Fouquet was poisoned by Louvois as they were former rivals.

The King wrote thus: "Move Lauzun to Fouquet's cell. Tell him that Dauger and La Rivière have been released."

Saint-Mars obeys his orders and moves Lauzun to Fouquet's cell.

The prisoner asks him and wonders if his release orders had come out.

But it wasn't going to be so fast.

"I am moving you to Fouquet's cell. Dauger and La Rivière have been released."

The prisoner did not show any surprise at the mention of Dauger's name. Saint-Mars confirmed his statements that he had known the existence of Dauger.

A poem written by Louis-Henri de Loménie de Brienne, an inmate in Saint-Lazare soon indicated that Eustache Dauger de Cavoye died because of heavy drinking in the late 1680s. Eustache Dauger de Cavoye was not involved in any way with the man in the mask.

It was the year 1681. Saint-Mars had received another instruction from the King. It concluded by saying: "Release Lauzun. "

Saint-Mars went to the room in which Lauzun was available and told him: "The king says that you can be released. "

He had earned his freedom.

That same year, Saint-Mars was appointed as the governor of the prison of the Exiles Fort.

Saint-Mars receives a scroll from the king. It read: "Take Dauger and the sick man, La Riviere with you when you start working as the governor of the prison of Exiles Fort. "

He escorts them to their respective cells.

Very soon, La Riviere meets his end. He dies in January 1687. From Exiles, the prisoner moves to the Îles in 1687.

There was absolute secrecy to which Dauger was condemned and the precaution of the mask. But now, Louvois becomes the man in the mask as a mark of his bitter enmity.

Again, there is a scroll that has landed from the King.

"Take Dauger with you. Let him wear an iron mask. All other arrangements including the cell having multiple doors should thus remain the same as before. "

Saint-Mars and Dauger thus move to Sainte-Marguerite, one of the Lerins Islands, half a mile offshore from Cannes.

Rumors spread as they journey. The current rumors are that there is a prisoner who is with the governor, and he doesn't have a face.

Saint-Mars reaches Lerins Islands and Dauger is placed in a cell with multiple doors.

Both guard and his prisoner had previously lived at the fortresses of Pignerol and Exiles in the Alps.

Duc de Beaufort's name was mentioned in a rumor begun by Saint-Mars in 1688.

Agents of the Dutch spread claims that the masked prisoner was a former lover of the queen's mother and was the king's real father—which would make Louis illegitimate.

It's the year 1698. The date is 18th September. Saint-Mars has a new post again. He is the governor of the Bastille prison in Paris. He has received a scroll from the king that the prisoner Dauger should be taken along with him. Saint-Mars does the king's bidding, a very obedient man, and he thus brings Dauger with him.

Once in prison, Eustache was at the mercy of Saint-Mars, who would enjoy fame and fortune as the jailer of illustrious prisoners.

Dauger is placed in a solitary cell. It's in the pre-furnished third chamber of the Bertaudiere tower.

Saint-Mars has a second in command who goes by the name de Rosaries. He was given the prime responsibility of feeding Dauger.

There was another officer on the rolls of this prison of Bastille. It was Lieutenant du Junca. He noticed that Dauger was a strange prisoner.

The masked prisoner died in Bastille prison on 19 November 1703. He was buried the next day under the name of "Marchialy" in the parish cemetery of Saint-Paul, and his age was "about 45."

This name resembled that of a former, more illustrious prisoner, suggesting that the wily Saint-Mars was still using pretense to boost his prestige.

It was the year 1711. King Louis's sister-in-law, Elizabeth Charlotte, Princess Palatine wrote a letter to her aunt, Sophia, Electress of Hanover. In one of the paragraphs, she mentioned the masked man. "There were rumors that the prisoner was always wearing a mask. He was not allowed to remove it. The prisoner was always guarded by two musketeers at his side. There were strict orders from Louis that they would kill him, even if there was a thought about removing the mask. The man in the mask was very devout. He was well treated and received everything that he desired. "

The man in the mask was already dead for eight years at that point. Elizabeth Charlotte had not seen him with her naked eyes. But she was citing the rumors that she had heard about the strange prisoner whenever she was at court.

"He was mysterious no doubt and the extent of the obvious precautions the jailers took for his sake, was appalling. There is significant interest in his story and my dear aunt I am not sure if I must call the prisoner a legend or whatever I am talking to you about is all coming from rumors that I have heard in court. "

"What could be the cause of his incarceration? Whatever I am hearing from people around me, does this kind of person exist or is it all based on embellished versions of an original tale? I feel sorry for this man, he must be having a very tough time, but he is, or he has been dealing with it incredibly well. Anyone else would just have gone hysterical by now, half crazy, half maniac. "

"Was he a Marshal of France, the English Henry Cromwell, son of Oliver Cromwell? Or was he Francois, Duke of Beaufort?"

In her reply to the Princess, the aunt describes some of her speculations about the man behind the mask. Sophia, the Electress of Hanover writes thus: "Could the man behind the mask be the son of Anne of Austria and Cardinal Mazarin? As he would thus be an illegitimate half-brother of Louis XIV, the king may want to hide him from the public. "

"Could he be Louis' twin brother who was born second, and hence younger of the two and was thrown into the prison to avoid any kind of dispute about who should hold the throne? But then, at the time that the king was born, there could have been controversy over which who came first, he or Louis."

"But then, I begin to wonder about the conditions of the childbirth for the queen mother. She's given birth in the presence of so many of the court's significant people. "

"Immediately after the birth of the present king, his father, Louis XIII had taken his whole court to the Chateau de Saint-German's chapel to celebrate a Te Deum. There was great pomp, and it was contrary to the common practice of celebrating it several days before the child was born. "

"There were several twin births before this, in the Capetian dynasty, as well as in the House of Valois, the House of Bourbon, and the House of Orleans to just cite a few examples. So, the possibility of the man in the mask being his twin is not ruled out. "

"Only two were proven tenable: Ercole Matthioli or Eustache Dauger."

"The enigmatic man spent several decades confined to the Bastille and other French prisons. "

"To Enlightenment thinkers, the masked man embodied the worst vices of King Louis XIV, depicted on this bronze medal."

"After his death, the unknown prisoner's story began to take on a life of its own as gossip said that his punishment stemmed directly from the French throne. "

However, Philippe creates his history in Spain as the Spanish ruler. Philippe the twin brother of the King becomes a towering figure. Crowned king of Spain, he rules the country gracefully. Aramis is at least truthful to one person and gives him the freedom that was denied to him at birth.

About the Author

D.S.Pais

D.S.Pais is an internationally acclaimed best-selling author. She is a born dreamer, imagines a lot, and has been writing since young. She is a creative person who previously worked as an actress in student films and TV series until she discovered that her passion was in writing. She writes short stories, novellas, novels, poetry, and self-help books, as she cannot put her thoughts anywhere else. When she is not working on a book, she enjoys reading books, watches movies, loves traveling, and routinely works out (Pilates) or other exercises. D.S.Pais works on several book titles and projects in a year and is very passionate about storytelling via words. Many of her titles have appeared among the top 100 Amazon Best Sellers in their section. Born and brought up in India, D.S. Pais is a Singaporean Citizen and lives in Singapore with her husband and two children.

YouTube Channel:

https://www.youtube.com/channel/UC3k5wx5eX2_alM0jo xJxk5g?sub_confirmation=1